RICHARD WRIGGLE

An Easy Peasy Person
from Easy Peasy Island
in the middle of the Terrific Ocean

Pan

Say hello to Richard Wriggle.
An Easy Peasy Island worm.
A worm in trouble.
You know how worms travel
around, don't you?
No, not by walking, because they
have no legs!
They wriggle.
But, as I will explain, that was
Richard Wriggle's trouble.
Richard lived on Easy Peasy
Island, down Strawberry Street, in
a hole.
An extremely comfortable hole.

Now, the trouble I was talking about, was that Richard Wriggle didn't know how to wriggle.
It should have been easy peasy, but, somehow or other, it just didn't seem to work.
Poor Richard Wriggle.
The only worm in the world who couldn't wriggle.

So, do you know how Richard Wriggle managed to get around Easy Peasy Island?

I'll tell you.

He hopped!

Richard Wriggle hopping was a sight to behold.

The only thing is that if you hop around all day, it hurts your tail.

HOP!

OUCH!

HOP, OUCH! HOP, OUCH! HOP!

One day, Richard was out for his afternoon walk.
Sorry. His afternoon hop.
HOP, OUCH! HOP, OUCH! HOP!
He met Shirley Chirp, an Easy Peasy bird.
"Hello, Richard," she called out cheerfully. "You don't look very happy!"
"In fact," she added, "you look perfectly unhappy!"

"My tail hurts," complained Richard Wriggle.

"That's because you're hopping on it," remarked Shirley.

"Why aren't you wriggling like worms are supposed to?"

"Can't," replied Richard.

"Well, if you can't wriggle, take a taxi," said Shirley, with a very birdy laugh.

And she went on her way, grinning an Easy Peasy birdy grin.

Richard Wriggle hopped on.
HOP, OUCH! HOP, OUCH! HOP!
He met Wizard Wheeze, the Easy
Peasy wizard, out for his afternoon
walk.
"Hopping hurts my tail,"
complained Richard.
"Worms don't hop," wheezed
Wizard Wheeze. "Worms wriggle!"
"Can't!" replied Richard, with a sad
wormy face.

Wizard Wheeze was just about to offer to help with some wizardy, wheezy, easy peasy magic when he remembered something.

He had left his magic umbrella at home!

So instead he said, "If you can't wriggle, catch a bus!"

Which wasn't very helpful.

And he laughed a very wizardy laugh, and went on his way, grinning an easy peasy wizardy grin.

Richard Wriggle hopped on.
HOP, OUCH! HOP, OUCH! HOP!
He met Charlie Oink, the Easy
Peasy pig.
"Hello, Richard," said Charlie, with
a smile. "What are you doing?"
"Hopping!" replied Richard
Wriggle.
Miserably.
"Worms don't hop," said Charlie
Oink. "Worms wriggle."
"Can't!" muttered Richard.
Even more miserably.

"Well," said Charlie Oink
cheerfully, "if you can't crawl . . ."
He thought for a moment.
"Take a train!"
And he laughed a very piggy
laugh, and went on his way,
grinning a very easy peasy piggy
grin.
Poor Richard Wriggle.
Nobody was being the least bit
nice to him, were they?

Richard Wriggle hopped on.
HOP, OUCH! HOP, OUCH! HOP!
He met Harry Hoof, the Easy Peasy
horse.
"Cheer up!" suggested Harry to
Richard Wriggle.
"Can't," came the sad reply. "My
tail hurts!"
"Well," replied Harry Hoof.
"Why don't you try wriggling
instead of hopping?"
Richard sighed a deep sigh.
"Can't," he mumbled.

Harry Hoof looked at him. And then he giggled.

"If you had a cart," he said, "I could pull it, and you could go everywhere by horse and cart!"

"Don't be silly," replied Richard Wriggle, getting annoyed.

So Harry Hoof went on his way laughing a very horsy laugh, and grinning a very easy peasy horsy grin.

Poor Richard Wriggle hopped unhappily home.

He curled up in his favourite armchair to think.

"It's no use," he thought to himself, "I'll have to learn."

And so he went outside to try.

"I WILL CRAWL!" he shouted.

"I WILL!

I WILL!

I WILL!"

But nobody was listening.

Oh, how he tried!
And tried again.
And then tried some more.
But the more he tried, the worse
it was.
He kept tying himself in knots!
He sighed a deep sigh.
But, in the middle of his sigh,
he had an idea.
A good idea.
A brilliant idea.
He laughed a very wormy laugh,
and grinned a very easy peasy
wormy grin.

And, do you know something?
These days Richard Wriggle gets
around Easy Peasy Island very
easily, thank you.
And his tail doesn't hurt from
hopping any more.
No more HOP, OUCH! HOP,
OUCH! HOP!
But can you guess how Richard
Wriggle gets around?
I'll tell you.

Instead of going for a walk, which he can't.
And instead of going for a wriggle, which he can't.
And instead of going for a hop, which hurts.
Do you know what he does?
It's easy peasy!
He simply turns himself into a circle, and he rolls.
He rolls!
I saw him yesterday.

Out for his Sunday afternoon roll!